MAHENDRA PAL ARYA

The Girl Beyond the Stars

BEYOND SPACE, BEYOND TIME

BLUEROSE PUBLISHERS
India | U.K.

Copyright © Mahendra Pal Arya 2025

All rights reserved by author. No part of this publication may be reproduced, stored in a retrieval system or transmitted in any form or by any means, electronic, mechanical, photocopying, recording or otherwise, without the prior permission of the author. Although every precaution has been taken to verify the accuracy of the information contained herein, the publisher assume no responsibility for any errors or omissions. No liability is assumed for damages that may result from the use of information contained within.

BlueRose Publishers takes no responsibility for any damages, losses, or liabilities that may arise from the use or misuse of the information, products, or services provided in this publication.

For permissions requests or inquiries regarding this publication, please contact:

BLUEROSE PUBLISHERS
www.BlueRoseONE.com
info@bluerosepublishers.com
+91 8882 898 898
+4407342408967

ISBN: 978-93-7139-458-1

Cover design: Daksh
Typesetting: Tanya Raj Upadhyay

First Edition: May 2025

Acknowledgment

Writing this book has been a journey of reflection, imagination, and persistence. I would like to express my heartfelt gratitude to those who supported me throughout this process.

First and foremost, I thank my mother, Vidhyawati Devi, whose love, strength, and blessings have been my guiding light.

To my entire family—your unwavering support has been my strength in every chapter of life. Your constant encouragement made this journey possible.

I am deeply grateful to my mentor, Dr. Barkha Rautela, for her insightful guidance and encouragement, and to my guide, Dr. Dharmveer Singh, for his invaluable support and direction during my research.

A special thanks to my dear friends Priya, Meera, Gaurav, and Megha, who walked beside me through every phase of this journey. Thank you for your patience, belief in my vision, and the warmth of your friendship.

— Mahendra Pal Arya

Table of Contents

Chapter 1: The Message from Beyond........ 1

Chapter 2: The First Discovery 10

Chapter 3: The Signal 20

Chapter 4: My Ignorance 30

Chapter 5: The Introduction 41

Chapter6: The Echo of Hope.......................... 50

Chapter 7: The Light of Silence 59

Chapter 8: The Research 93

Chapter 9: The Loops of Xelora.................... 100

Chapter 10: The Instantaneous Light 111

Chapter 11: The Impossible Choice........... 122

Chapter 12: The Final Light.......................... 131

Chapter 1:
The Message from Beyond

Life gives you purpose with the entangling streets. I found a machine behind the wall, it says, "Wait for the time".

After some years -

It was a quiet night on Earth when I first saw her — a small, fragile figure standing alone in an alien planet's cold, barren landscape. The night sky stretched infinitely above, a canvas of stars scattered like diamonds across the deep black void. I sat in front of the large telescope at the observatory, the chill of the late evening air creeping in through the cracks in the window. I had been waiting for this moment for years—the first glimpse of a new star system. The latest discoveries had shown a planet in the distant systems, 50 light-years away, and a world I had been studying for months. But tonight was different. Tonight, I saw something impossible.

At first, the telescope's focus seemed normal—stars, nebulae, dark voids between galaxies—the usual. But as I turned the dial and adjusted the focus, something unexpected appeared on the screen—a figure, small and distinct, moving across a strange landscape.

My breath caught in my throat. I leaned in closer to the eyepiece. There was someone there.

A girl, no older than fifteen, stood on a planet far beyond our reach. She was wearing a tattered cloak that flapped lightly in the wind, her hair wild and unkempt, as though she had been running for days. In the dim, pale light from the distant star, her face looked tired, desperate, yet determined. She stood near an ancient, broken fountain without water surrounded by large, gnarled trees with twisted trunks and glowing leaves. The sky above her was a deep violet hue, and a faint mist hovered around the ground, like smoke rising from a forgotten fire.

I blinked, adjusting the telescope's lenses again. What was I looking at? My heart began to race. The girl's image was not static; she moved, her silhouette shifting in the strange wind that swirled around her. But what struck me most was the eerie silence. The image was too clear, too vivid, almost as if she were standing in front of me. I could almost feel her presence, like she was right there, beyond the lens.

I instinctively checked the telescope's equipment. Everything was in perfect order, with no glitches or malfunctions.

But what I was seeing should not have been possible. I was looking at a world 50 light-years away. The light from that planet—even travelling at the speed of light—would have taken 50 years to reach Earth. The girl, if she existed, should have been long gone. The image I was seeing should have been from the past.

But the strange thing was, it wasn't from the past. It is present.

I hesitated momentarily, trying to convince myself that I was imagining things. Perhaps it was some visual artifact, a trick of the telescope. Maybe the equipment was playing tricks on me, or there was some error in the signal transmission. I checked again, ensuring the settings were correct. But there was no denying it. The image of the girl before me was as real as anything I had ever seen.

The camera's feed was steady, but as I adjusted the zoom in closer, I saw something that sent a chill down my spine: the girl was holding a piece of paper in her hand.

It fluttered slightly in the wind, and she held it tightly, as though it were her only lifeline. But it wasn't the paper that captured my attention. It was her expression. She was staring directly at me — at the lens, as if she knew I was there, watching. Her eyes locked with mine, and for a brief, surreal moment, it felt like time had stopped. I couldn't look away.

The moment stretched on, longer than it should have. She stepped forward, her body slightly jerking as though she had been running for too long. And then, in a moment of horror, her lips parted. She screamed, but the sound didn't reach me. Her mouth opened wide, her face twisted in what looked like pure terror, yet all I could hear was silence.

I froze. I've spent years in the observatory, tracking distant stars and studying distant galaxies, but I had never felt something so visceral. Her scream should have been impossible to hear, considering the distance. Yet, somehow, I thought it — deep in my chest. Her scream was a silent plea, a cry that resonated across the stars, tearing through the fabric of space, and pulling at something inside me.

My hands trembled as I adjusted the focus, desperate for a clearer view of her. What was happening? Who was she? And why was she trapped in that distant world?

Her scream echoed in my mind as I zoomed in on her hand, where she clutched the piece of paper. She held it up toward the sky, her fingers trembling, almost like she was begging for someone — for me — to see it. I adjusted the view finder one final time, hoping to read the message.

And there it was, written in bold, neat handwriting:

"HELP ME. TIME IS SLIPPING AWAY."

I couldn't breathe. Time is slipping away? What did she mean by that? This girl, standing alone on a distant planet, was sending me a message — now, in real-time. But how was this possible? How could she be sending this message across 50 light-years?

I felt a chill crawl down my spine. The message was clear, and it was meant for me. But how was I seeing it? The light from Xelora, where she was, would have taken 50 years to reach Earth. Yet the message was real-time. I saw her now, not a moment from the past, but her present. How was that even possible? I reached for my notebook and scribbled down everything I had seen, my mind racing with questions. Was it a coincidence? Was this some malfunction with the telescope? Maybe I was just tired, my mind playing tricks on me. But deep down, I knew something wasn't right. This wasn't just an image — it was a connection.

I pulled out my phone and called Dr. Matthew, the head of the observatory. Her voice was groggy, clearly startled by the late-night call, but I didn't care.

"Dr. Matthew, you need to come down here," I said, trying to keep my voice steady. "I've seen something... something impossible."

When she arrived, I showed her the telescope feed. The girl was still there, standing by the rocks, holding the paper, her eyes wide with fear. Dr. Matthews stared at the screen silently for several long moments, and then turned to me with a look of disbelief.

"This... this can't be real," she whispered. "If what you're telling me is true, then what we're seeing — this girl, this message — would violate everything we know about physics. You can't see the present from 50 light-years away. Light from her planet should take decades to reach us. Yet we're seeing her in real-time, now."

I nodded. I didn't need her to tell me what I already knew. This wasn't a glitch. This was real. But the question remained: How?

Chapter 2:
The First Discovery

Dr. Matthews was astonished, as anyone would be. We stood in the dark, quiet observatory, the machines' soft hum and clocks ticking in the background. But none of that mattered. We were focused on one impossible thing — the image on the screen. The girl was standing in the distant world of Xelora, 50 light-years away. And somehow, impossibly, she was reaching out to me now.

As I stared at the screen, I struggled to process what I saw. The girl was real — her eyes wide with fear, her hands gripping the piece of paper so tightly it looked like she might tear it. The landscape behind her, with its alien brown rocks, was just as tangible, just as present. But it couldn't be.

The laws of physics told me it couldn't be, yet here it was.

Xelora was a world beyond reach, far away, hidden in the depths of space. I had been studying many planets for weeks using the latest telescopic technology to observe distant star systems, except this one single Planet, which I considered nothing. I had expected to see data on stars, planets, and galaxies — things I had seen many times before. But nothing had prepared me for this.

Light, as we understand it, travels at a constant speed: approximately 300,000 kilometres per second. This speed, though immense, is still finite. That's why, when we observe distant stars, we see them not as they are right now, but as when their light began its journey to Earth. The further away a star is, the older the light we see. The light from Xelora should have taken 50 years to reach Earth. That's how far the Planet was from us — 50 light-years.

But here I was, staring at a real-time image of the girl, her face full of desperation. The date on the paper she was holding — March 5, 2024 — was the exact same date I saw on my calendar in the observatory. This wasn't just an image from the past. This was happening now. Dr. Matthew was lost in some equations on the board, but nothing worked for this amazement.

I double-checked the equipment. I adjusted the telescope's focus, making sure the lenses were correctly calibrated. I ran diagnostics on the computer systems, scanning for errors or malfunctions. There were no issues, no glitches. The image was clear. There were no distortions, no signs of artifacting. The girl's form was crisp, her features sharply defined, the landscape behind her glowing eerily under the pale light of a distant star.

I leaned back in my chair, trying to breathe through the mounting tension. It was as if the concept of time was being tested in front of my eyes. I studied Einstein's theories of special and general relativity for years. I understood the idea of time dilation, how gravity could bend space-time, and how light could be delayed over vast distances. But none of that explained what I was seeing. There was no way this could be happening.

I turned to Dr. Matthews, who had now been standing silently beside me, her face pale, her eyes fixed on the screen. She had mentored me, a brilliant astrophysicist with years of experience. If anyone could help me make sense of this, it was her. But she wasn't speaking. She just stared, her mouth slightly open, as though waiting for some explanation to emerge.

"Doctor…" I finally spoke, my voice trembling slightly. "This… this can't be real. How is this possible? I'm looking at her, and it's… happening now."

Dr. Matthews blinked, as if she had just been jolted out of a trance. "I… I don't know," she said softly, her voice low and strained. "I've never seen anything like this. The laws of physics, the way we understand them, say this shouldn't be happening. Light from that Planet should have taken 50 years to reach us. But what you're seeing is happening right now. In real-time."

Her words echoed in my mind, but they didn't make sense. How could something like this exist? A signal—an image—from 50 light-years away, in real time? The implications were staggering. If what we were witnessing was true, then we were seeing something that defied everything we thought we knew about space and time.

I focused again on the girl. Her lips were still moving, but this time she sat down, and there was no sound — of course, there couldn't be. Sound doesn't travel through the vacuum of space. Yet somehow, her mouth opened wide in a silent scream, a scream I could almost hear in my mind. Her face twisted in a silent plea for help, her eyes staring directly into the telescope lens. It was as though she knew we were watching her, as though she could sense the pull of our attention from across the vast gulf of space.

And then, there was the paper.

The piece of paper she was holding up toward the sky fluttered slightly in the breeze of her alien world, the words written on it unmistakable:

"HELP ME. TIME IS SLIPPING AWAY."

Those words were clear. The message was urgent and pleading, and it was being sent from her present **to** my present. The strangest thing of all was that the date on the paper — March 5, 2024 — was identical to the date on the clock in the observatory.

My head spun as I tried to understand. Was it possible that I was looking at a transmission of some kind, a signal sent by the girl that had taken 50 years to travel through space? That would explain the distance. But it didn't explain how I could see her present, not an image of her past. The light was arriving from a point in space 50 years ago, but what I saw wasn't an image of the girl 50 years ago. It was her, now. Right now.

I felt a deep, gnawing panic settle in the pit of my stomach. The message on the paper was clear: Time is slipping away, **but** slipping away from what? And from whom? Dr. Matthew asks, "Who sent her there and when?"

We decided to focus on the problem; Dr. Matthews and I both understood its core. Time, as we understood it, is a linear progression—a steady march from past to present to future. The light from Xelora should have been from the past—from 50 years ago, from the time when the light first left her Planet. But what we were seeing was now happening in real time.

I ran through every possible theory in my mind. Was there some gravitational anomaly near Xelora that could have bent space-time, allowing us to see her image in real-time? We had heard of phenomena like this before, in the form of gravitational lensing, where light from distant objects is bent around massive objects like black holes or neutron stars, allowing us to see distant objects in distorted, magnified ways. However, the problem with this theory was that the image was too clear. There was no distortion. No bending. Just a perfect, crystal-clear picture.

There was also the possibility of a wormhole, a theoretical passage through space-time that could connect two distant points in the universe. If such a thing existed between Earth and Xelora, it would allow us to see her in real-time. But again, this was pure speculation. We had never detected anything like that near Xelora.

Dr. Matthews finally spoke, her voice tinged with disbelief. "This... this isn't just a glitch or some distortion. The data from the telescope is solid. There's nothing wrong with the equipment. The light from

Xelora is somehow reaching us in real-time. But how? How can that be possible?"

I shook my head, my mind spinning. I had no answer. I only knew one thing: the girl on Xelora, her message, and the strange connection we had with her were real, and something was very wrong in her world. I watched her again, her hand shaking as she clutched the paper. Was she trapped there? Was she alone? And why was she reaching out to me, across 50 light-years, asking for help?

The questions were endless, and the answers, so far, were nonexistent. But one thing was sure: we had to find out what was happening on Xelora. Time — her time — was slipping away.

Chapter 3:
The Signal

As days turned into weeks, my fixation with the girl on Xelora only intensified. I found myself unable to tear my eyes away from the telescope, constantly monitoring the screen that seemed to tether me to a distant world. She vanished during the day, but each night, I found myself drawn to her once more, the girl I had grown familiar with through the lens of my telescope. There was a new depth in her eyes, a hint of something beyond fear. It was desperation, but it was also something more — a sense of awareness. Despite the vast expanse between us, she was aware of my gaze.

When I first saw her, standing alone in the strange, barren valley, her scream had been pure anguish. She had been isolated, alone, and terrified, her eyes filled with the kind of terror that comes from facing the unknown. But throughout the following nights, something changed. The image I saw of her was no longer just a reflection of an unfortunate girl stranded on a faraway planet. Dr. Matthew has decided not to pay attention to it, but I know she will go through it.

Her expression shifted. The fear was still there, but now, in its place, was something far more profound — a call for help, a plea for salvation.

I had no evidence, no scientific explanation, but deep within me, I could feel it: she knew I was watching her. There was no logical reason for this, and no theory in the physics textbooks I had studied could account for such a thing. How could she know? And why was she now so intent on communicating with me?

The more I observed, the clearer her intentions became. The piece of paper she clutched became a symbol, a way for her to send messages across the unbridgeable gulf of space and time. Each time I saw her hold the paper, she had written more — her words were growing more urgent and direct. At first, the messages were cryptic, fleeting, like whispers across the void. But soon, she began writing in a way that mirrored my own present time on Earth as though she were aware of the passing days and the exact date.

As I delved deeper into her messages, a profound sense of responsibility began to weigh on me. It felt as if I were the only one who could answer her call. My rational mind screamed that it was impossible, that this was nothing but an illusion, a trick of the mind. But the part of me that had spent countless hours studying the stars and listening to the universe's silent hum knew that something inexplicable was happening. What about the Doctor? She has also seen her. I was sure my mind was playing games with me.

My focus shifted to deciphering her messages, every detail on the piece of paper, every flicker of her form in the telescope's view. But the more I delved into it, the more questions surfaced. How could she be writing the exact date, the same time, and in a way that seemed synchronised with Earth's time? How was it possible for her, trapped on a planet 50 light-years away, to write in a manner that mirrored the Earth's present? The mystery only deepened.

Then, it happened. One night, as I sat at the telescope, the flickering static on the receiver suddenly changed. It was faint at first, just a whisper against the hum of the equipment, a blip in the usual noise of the telescope. But something told me that this was different. I adjusted the receiver, heart pounding, fingers trembling as I tuned the signal. The static was almost imperceptible, like the soft sound of distant winds in a storm.

But then, it grew stronger.

The crackling sound that had been nothing more than a distant murmur transformed into something I could almost hear. I could feel my breath catch in my throat. The words began to emerge, distorted at first, like voices struggling through thick fog. They were hard to make out, scrambled, yet undeniably real. The signal was coming from **Xelora**, the planet I had been observing.

I leaned forward, the blood rushing to my head. The words finally emerged from the static, clearer now, but still faint. I held my breath, straining to catch each word:

"Help me. Time is slipping away."

My heart stopped.

I blinked, my mind struggling to process what I was hearing. The signal had come from her. The girl on Xelora. It was as though she had somehow found a way to send this message directly to me, to reach me across time and space. I had no idea how it was possible — no equipment capable of transmitting such a signal, no technology that could communicate across light-years of space. The distance alone should have made this impossible. How could it be happening? How could she be sending this signal?

I sat back, staring at the screen. The words echoed in my mind, and a cold chill crept up my spine. How was this happening? It didn't make sense. I had no way of explaining it. All I had was the signal itself — a message, a plea from across the vast space, directly addressing me.

I was alone in the observatory, but the feeling of isolation had never been stronger. It was as if I were standing on the edge of the universe, looking into an unknown beyond comprehension. The girl, standing on her distant planet, had sent her message. And I had received it. There was no mistaking it. It wasn't a trick of the equipment. This was something real that defied the boundaries of science and reason.

For the longest time, I had thought that the telescope was just a tool, a way to observe the universe from a distance. But now, it felt like something far more profound. It was a bridge, a way to connect to something or someone, far beyond my reach. I had been trying to understand how the girl could send real-time messages. Was this some technology that allowed for instantaneous transmission across space? Was this some form of quantum entanglement, a phenomenon that allows particles to be connected in ways that don't obey the standard rules of physics?

I didn't know. My rational side screamed for an explanation, for some scientific reasoning, something I could understand and quantify. But the other side, the one that had spent years gazing into the night sky, knowing that there was more to the universe than we could understand, knew this was something beyond anything we had ever conceived.

I leaned forward and began typing rapidly, recording the signal on my equipment. I had to document everything. I had to find a way to preserve this moment, to prove that it had happened. But even as I typed, my mind raced. Was there a way to respond to her? Could I send a message back to Xelora? I had no idea how, but the thought consumed me. Time was slipping away, she had said. What if she were running out of time? What if this was her final plea?

The more I thought about it, the more I understood — I couldn't just observe anymore. This was no longer just an academic exercise. This was real. She was real. And she was asking for help.

But how could I help? How could I, here on Earth, aid a girl on a planet 50 light-years away? As we understood them, the laws of physics didn't offer any solutions. I couldn't even begin to fathom how she was sending a signal, let alone how I could respond. Yet there was something I could do. I could keep watching. I could keep recording. I could keep trying to decipher the messages, trying to understand what she was going through and experiencing.

The girl's cry for help was no longer just a distant sound in the dark corners of space. It was a call that echoed deep within me, challenging everything I knew. I wasn't just a scientist looking at distant stars anymore. I had become part of the story. Her story.

And I wouldn't let it end without doing everything I could to help.

Chapter 4:
My Ignorance

The days blurred into one another in a ceaseless wave of indifference. Time had a way of folding itself in on me, bending the hours into an endless repetition that seemed to exist only in the spaces between the signals — the faint transmissions from Xelora that haunted the periphery of my work, mind, and life. I would have been lying if I said I didn't hear them. The static, faint whispers, and cries for help grew more urgent each time. But I ignored them. I ignored *her*.

It wasn't that I didn't care. It wasn't that I wasn't bothered by the disembodied voice of a girl crying for help from across the universe. No, it was that I couldn't afford to care. I had work to do, research to focus on, and answers to find — answers that would never come from staring into the void of space and listening to a girl's helpless pleas. I wasn't a hero. I was a scientist, trained to observe, study, and decipher the known. The unknown was too much. Too *impossible*.

The first transmission had come to me like a whisper in the dark. Her scream had pierced through the usual static, and I had thought it was a glitch — a momentary disturbance in the equipment. But then, after a few more nights, I couldn't deny it was real. She was real. I could see her through the lens of my telescope, standing alone in a barren valley on Xelora, her eyes wide with fear, her body stiff with the kind of isolation only a person lost in the deepest parts of space could know. She was begging for help.

"Help me. Time is slipping away."

That was the first message I had heard. It echoed in my ears long after the transmission faded into the static. How could she know? How could a girl, stranded fifty light-years away, send such a message to me, to *Earth*? There was no logical explanation or scientific theory to explain the phenomenon. But the girl, the image of her standing alone under a desolate sky, was real. And that scared me more than I cared to admit.

I couldn't pull myself away from the telescope for a few nights. The world outside of the observatory ceased to matter as I focused on the screen, on her. She wasn't just a dot on the display anymore — she was a presence, a soul, a being that somehow transcended the vast gulf of space and time. It was as though she was speaking directly to me, as though she *knew* I was watching. But how? It didn't make sense. Nothing about it made sense.

Each night, I studied her, desperate to find an answer and a way to understand what was happening. The messages from her grew more direct, more hopeless. The piece of paper she clutched had become a symbol, an object that seemed to contain her cries, thoughts, and pleas for help. She wrote more now, each message growing clearer, more precise, as though she were aware of the passing days on Earth — aware of the exact time and date. It was impossible. How could she know?

And yet, despite the confusion and mounting questions, I couldn't stop myself. I became consumed by her. It wasn't just a scientific curiosity anymore. It was something far more profound, far more personal.

But then, as time passed, the uncertainty began to eat away at me. Dr. Matthew, my colleague and the voice of reason in my life, had dismissed my concerns. "You're letting your mind run wild," he had said, the usual condescension in his voice. "There's no way this could be real. It's a distortion, a glitch in the equipment. You've got to focus on the data, on the facts."

His words, so cold and detached, began to feel like a lifeline, a safety net I clung to, to protect myself from the unravelling truth. I didn't want to believe it. I didn't want to think that there was something beyond the laws of physics, beyond what science could explain. It was easier to convince myself that it was a trick of the mind. It was just another mystery in the cosmos that I didn't need to waste time unravelling.

And so I stopped. I stopped looking at the signals, searching the screen for her image, and listening to her voice.

It was easy at first. I focused on my work, burying myself in the research I had set aside. I told myself I had to concentrate on the practical, the tangible. The girl from Xelora became just another part of the noise, another irrelevant detail in the grand scale of the universe. I convinced myself that I was doing the right thing. After all, what could I do? What was the point of trying to save someone trapped on a planet light-years away? It was *impossible*. It couldn't be done.

But no matter how hard I tried, I couldn't shake the feeling that I was lying to myself. The guilt started to creep in, slowly at first, a faint discomfort that I could ignore. But it grew.

I began to feel like a coward. I knew she was out there, waiting for help, and yet I continued to turn away. I could hear the static in the background sometimes, the faint murmurs of a transmission coming through, but I refused to listen.

Dr. Matthew had been right, I told myself. There was no reason to get caught up in something so irrational. The signals were just noise. The girl wasn't real. She was just a figment of my overactive imagination. She was nothing more than an anomaly, a glitch. And I—I was smarter than that. I knew better than to get caught up in some impossible, emotional fantasy.

But no matter how much I tried to convince myself, I couldn't escape the nagging feeling that I was wrong. I had spent years studying the stars, galaxies, and the vast expanse of the universe. I had spent hours peering into the darkness, seeking answers to questions that no one had ever thought to ask. But this-this girl, her cries, her messages—was something I couldn't explain away. It was something that gnawed at my conscience every moment of every day.

One evening, after weeks of silence, I finally gave in. I sat down at the telescope, my hands trembling as I adjusted the equipment, as if I could somehow avoid looking at the screen — avoid seeing her again. But there she was, standing in the same barren valley, the same piece of paper clutched in her hands. And the message she had written this time was not cryptic. It wasn't vague.

"Why aren't you helping me?" The words flickered across the screen, sharp and accusing. "You've watched. You've waited. But you've done nothing. Why?"

I froze. My heart thudded painfully in my chest. It was as though she could hear my thoughts, sense my indecision, my reluctance. It wasn't just a plea anymore. It was an accusation. She was holding me accountable.

I felt the weight of her words press down on me, heavy and suffocating. How could I have ignored her for so long? How could I have just walked away, pretending that it wasn't real, that I wasn't the one she was reaching out to? She wasn't some distant observer to me anymore. She wasn't just a data point in an experiment. She was a person. She was someone who was *suffering*, and I had turned my back on her.

The truth hit me like a cold wave, and I recoiled from it. I hadn't just been ignoring the girl on Xelora. I had been ignoring the very essence of what it meant to be human. She had contacted me, and I had refused to acknowledge it. I had refused to even *try*.

I wanted to stop. I tried to shut it all down, to forget her, to bury her in the depths of my mind where I could pretend she didn't exist. But I couldn't. Her message had cracked through the facade I had built around myself, and now there was no way to hide from it.

I wanted to scream, to shout at the universe for giving me this impossible burden. How could I help her? How could I answer her call when everything in the world told me it was beyond my reach? The girl on Xelora wasn't a hero's story. She was a tragedy. And I had chosen to ignore it.

The static started again, faint at first, a low hum coming from nowhere. My fingers hovered over the controls, but I didn't move. I just stared at the screen, at her, as her words faded into nothing.

And in that moment, I realised the true nature of my ignorance: I wasn't just ignoring her. I was ignoring myself. I had shut off my humanity, my connection to the world, because it was easier than facing the truth. It was easier to pretend that it was all some cosmic mistake, some anomaly of the universe.

But that didn't make it any less real.

She was real. And I had failed her.

As the signal disappeared into the void once more, I knew that nothing was left for me but the weight of my own inaction. I had chosen to turn away, and in doing so, I had severed the last thread.

Chapter 5:
The Introduction

I sat in my apartment's small, cluttered office, the dim light from a single desk lamp casting a soft, yellow glow over the chaos of papers, books, and research journals scattered across my desk. The room smelled faintly of coffee and old textbooks, the scent that could only mean long nights spent in the company of equations and observations. My vintage telescope, which I had prized since I was a graduate student, loomed in the corner of the room. Once, it had been my primary connection to the stars, the galaxies, and the vast cosmos beyond our planet. Now, it stood as a monument to my obsession — a silent reminder of the scientific pursuit I had dedicated my life to, and yet, these days, it was rarely used.

At 28, I had already made a name for myself in astrophysics. I'd spent years studying celestial bodies, galaxies, and the fundamental mysteries of the universe. My research had contributed to groundbreaking discoveries, and I was known for my ability to make sense of data, to find patterns and correlations where others saw only confusion. I had built my career on cold logic and scientific precision, distancing myself from the more unpredictable aspects of life. My colleagues respected me for my intellect, but they knew little about me outside of my work. My personal life, or lack thereof, was a mystery — not to them, but to me.

I wasn't one to make waves or seek attention. I found comfort in solitude, in the quiet moments spent in my office or the isolation of the observatory. People, relationships, connections — they were all things that I had never really known how to handle. But there was one person who had always made me feel more, even if I could never bring myself to say it. Her name was Catherine.

I met her years ago during my postdoctoral years. We had been paired together for a research project that combined astrophysics and atmospheric studies, and from the moment we started working together, something about her intrigued me. She was brilliant, compassionate, and incredibly insightful. But it wasn't just her intellect that drew me in. It was how she saw the world — the warmth she exuded, the way she connected with everyone around her. Catherine had this effortless ability to make people feel seen and valued, and in some quiet, unspoken way that captivated me from the beginning.

I loved her.

But I had never told her.

I never could.

I was not afraid, but I respect her as just a friend. It was easier to keep my emotions buried, to convince myself that she was better off without me. I was a scientist, not a lover. I could study the stars, but couldn't navigate the complexity of human relationships. So, I did what I could. Every few months, whenever I felt I must call, I would reach out to her — a brief phone call to check in. To hear her voice.

"Hey, Catherine," I would say, my voice steady, controlled. "I thought I'd check in, see how you're doing. I know it's been a while, but I wanted to ensure you're alright."

It was always the same. A short, polite call asking about her and the family: I always say, "Someday I will come to meet you", and then I'd hang up the phone, the silence settling over me again. Each time, the conversation ended before I could say what I felt or tell her what was in my heart. It was not necessary to speak to her. So I kept my distance, content with the occasional call, letting the unspoken words linger in the space between us.

But that was all I had. It was all I knew how to do.

And then, there was the girl from Xelora.

The first time I encountered the signal from Xelora, I thought it was just a glitch — some interference in the data — a miscalculation, perhaps, or a quirk in the equipment. But as the signal persisted, something in me refused to let it go. The data was different. The signal had a rhythm, a pattern too specific to be dismissed as noise. And then, when I saw the girl on the screen, her face filled with fear and desperation, something inside me snapped.

She wasn't just a figure on a distant planet. She was real. She was reaching out, and somehow, I was the one she was calling to. I couldn't explain it. The science didn't add up. The laws of physics, the things I had built my career upon, didn't allow for such a connection. And yet, I couldn't deny it. The girl from Xelora had sent a message—a cry for help.

Now I do not return to the telescope to study her image; I only search for any hint of an explanation. Because every time I saw her, it was as though she knew I was watching her. Her eyes, filled with fear and sorrow, seemed to lock with mine through the lens, as if we shared some unspoken bond. The messages she sent — cryptic at first, but becoming more urgent with each passing day — grew harder to ignore. "Help me," she had written. "Time is slipping away."

I couldn't stop thinking about her. How could I? Here was someone—someone I didn't know, someone from a world fifty light-years away — reaching out for help, and I was the only one who could hear her. The rational part of me told me it was impossible. There was no way a signal could travel such a vast distance in real-time, no way that this could be anything other than some strange, unexplainable anomaly. But the part of me that had spent years studying the stars and always looked for connections between the known and the unknown couldn't shake the feeling that this was something important.

Something that couldn't be ignored.

And yet, I found myself torn between two worlds. On one hand, there was

Catherine — the woman I had loved for years, the woman I had never told how I felt. And on the other, there was the girl from Xelora — a voice calling to me from the depths of space. The universe had thrown me a curveball, a dilemma I didn't know how to handle.

Catherine deserves someone who belongs to her community, who could be present for her in a way I never could. She deserves someone who could give her the kind of attention and affection I had never been able to offer. But now, in the face of the girl from Xelora, I was again caught in indecision. Could I help her? Could I reach out to her across the impossible distance of space? Or was this all just a figment of my imagination, a trick of my mind?

I spent sleepless nights staring at the screen, watching the girl from Xelora's every move, every word. But as the days stretched on, my thoughts began to spiral. She consumed me. And at the same time, I couldn't stop thinking about Catherine. Sometimes I feel so low without her and ask myself - How could I have let so many years go by without telling her what I truly felt?

And now, the girl from Xelora had entered my life, demanding my attention, pulling me into a mystery I wasn't sure I could solve. But even as I became increasingly obsessed with the signal from Xelora, I couldn't help but wonder: was I capable of loving anyone? Could I ever take that leap with Catherine, or was I destined to remain a passive observer in my own life, never truly taking action?

The universe had thrown me into an impossible situation. And for the first time, I wasn't sure which direction to take.

Chapter 6:
The Echo of Hope

The night of my ignorance lingered like a wound that refused to heal. The guilt gnawed at me, a relentless tide that eroded the walls I had built to keep the world at bay. But something in me broke that evening, and with trembling hands, I found myself at the telescope again. Xelora loomed on the screen, its barren valleys stretching into a desolate horizon. And there she was — or rather, where she had been. The girl lay crumpled on the ground, her form a fragile shadow against the cold light of the distant star. The paper she had once clutched so tightly was now strewn beside her, lifeless and forgotten. My heart sank like a stone in a dark ocean. The void between us had never felt so vast. I screamed her name, though I had never known it. My voice, hoarse and desperate, echoed in the empty observatory. The girl didn't stir. The screen showed no movement, no signs of life. The air around me seemed to thicken with despair, the static from the speakers hissing like a cruel taunt. I had waited too long. I had ignored her cries for help, and now she is gone. A wild panic overtook me. My hands flew across the controls, recalibrating, fine-tuning, and searching for any sign of life. My fingers trembled, sweat beading on my brow. The signal flickered, unstable, as though mocking my efforts. But I refused to give up. Not now. Not when she needed me. "Please," I whispered, my voice cracking. "Please, don't let it end like this." And then, the faintest twitch. A finger moved, barely perceptible, but enough to send a jolt of hope surging through me. Her arm shifted, weak and hesitant, as though struggling against the weight of a thousand galaxies. She was alive. She was alive! I let out a shuddering breath, relief crashing over me like a tidal wave. But the victory was short-lived. She wasn't moving enough. Her body remained limp, her movements feeble, and the hollow emptiness in her eyes was a void that no amount of light could fill. She was alive, but she wasn't speaking. She wasn't responding. I screamed into the receiver, desperate for her to hear me and know she wasn't alone. "Can you hear me?" I shouted, my voice raw with urgency. "You're not alone! I'm here! Please, say something!" But there was no answer because she couldn't hear me. Her lips didn't move. Her body remained still except for the occasional tremor, a fragile echo of vitality. I felt a surge of frustration, of helplessness. The vast distance between us was a chasm I couldn't cross, no matter how desperately I wished to. In my mind, a war raged. I was a scientist, bound by the laws of physics, by the cold, unyielding truths of the universe. But this wasn't science anymore. This was raw and visceral, a connection defying logic and reason. She was real. Her pain was real. And I couldn't turn away again. I redoubled my efforts. The paper she had dropped caught my eye, its edges fluttering faintly in an unseen wind. Zooming in, I tried to make out the words scrawled across its surface. The writing was faint and smudged, but legible enough to piece together: Time is slipping away. Find me. The words burned into my mind, a haunting reminder of her desperation. What did she mean by "time slipping away"? Was it a cry for rescue? A warning? Or something more profound, something tied to the very fabric of reality itself? Hours passed. I worked feverishly, combing through data, analysing the signal, searching for a way to bridge the impossible gap. Sleep was a distant memory, an indulgence I couldn't afford. My focus narrowed to a singular goal: saving her. I didn't care about its impossibility. I didn't care about the questions that would come later. All that mattered was her survival. The static in the background shifted a subtle change in frequency that sent a shiver down my spine. It was as though the universe itself was holding its breath, waiting. The screen flickered, and for a moment, her eyes met mine. They were hollow, but there was something there — a spark, a glimmer of recognition. "You're not alone," I whispered again, my voice trembling. "I'm here. I'll find a way. I promise." The connection faltered, the signal wavering. Her image blurred, the edges dissolving into the void. I slammed my fist against the console, a surge of anger and frustration boiling over. The universe wasn't fair. It never had been. But I couldn't let it win. Not this time. And then, as if in answer to my silent plea, she moved again. Her hand, weak and trembling, reached for the paper. She lifted it, holding it out toward the lens. The words were clearer now, etched desperately: Help me. You're my only hope. The weight of those words crushed me. I wasn't a hero. I wasn't someone who could defy the laws of the universe, who could leap across the stars to save her. But in her eyes, I was all she had. And that was enough. I spent the rest of the night devising a plan. It was reckless, impossible even, but I didn't care. I would take it if there were even the slightest chance of reaching her. I combed through every piece of data, every fragment of information I had gathered over the weeks. Patterns emerged, faint and elusive, like the threads of a tapestry waiting to be woven together. By dawn, I had a theory. It wasn't much and relied on assumptions bordering on fantasy. But it was all I had. The signals she had sent weren't just cries for help. They were coordinates, encoded in the static, hidden in the layers of noise. If I could decode them, I might be able to locate her exact position on Xelora. The thought made my heart race. Resources and experimental technologies had been dismissed as impractical and theoretical. But at this moment, practicality didn't matter. I began drafting messages to every contact I had in the field, calling in favours, pulling strings. The stakes were too high for hesitation. The hours blurred into days, each moment a step closer to an impossible goal. The girl's image remained burned into my mind, constantly reminding me why I couldn't stop. Sleep was a luxury I couldn't afford. Food was an afterthought. My world had shrunk to the size of a screen and a signal, and nothing else mattered. And then, one night, as I pieced together the final fragments of the encoded message, the signal shifted again. Her voice, faint and trembling, broke through the static: "Time... slipping... away..." It was barely a whisper, but it was enough. She was still there. Still holding on. And so would I. The universe was vast, cruel, and indifferent. But in the face of that enormity, there was a spark of hope, fragile and flickering but real. I wouldn't let it die. This wasn't just about saving her anymore. It was about proving that humanity could reach out and make a difference even in the cold, unfeeling void of space. It was about defying the impossible, about finding a way where none existed. As I stared into the screen, her eyes met mine once more. And at that moment, I knew I would do whatever it took. For the fragile thread of connection that bound us across the stars. The night stretched on, and the journey ahead seemed insurmountable. But I wasn't alone anymore. Neither was she. And together, we would find a way.

Chapter 7:
The Light of Silence

The questions swirled in my mind as I stared at the flickering screen. How could she still be alive? How could she communicate with me across the unfathomable void of space? According to every scan and report, Xelora was barren, devoid of any breathable atmosphere or life-supporting elements. The stars, distant and indifferent, offered no answers. The girl was somewhere on that desolate surface, but her presence defied all logic.

The signals she had sent were a mystery in them—encoded, layered with noise, and yet infused with a precision that suggested intelligence far beyond mere coincidence. The coordinates, embedded in those signals, were precise now, marking a location deep within one of Xelora's endless valleys. But even with that clarity, the enigma of her existence remained. How was she surviving? And more perplexing, how was she speaking to me, reaching me across the unimaginable chasm of space?

I leaned back in my chair, rubbing my temples as exhaustion tugged at me. The observatory was silent save for the faint hum of equipment, a stark contrast to the turmoil in my mind. I needed answers; understanding the planet itself was the only way to get them.

Hours stretched into an unrecognizable blur of data and analysis. The steady hum of machinery filled the space, punctuated only by the soft whir of the control panel and the rhythmic pulse of the monitors. My fingers moved across the keyboard in a blur as I navigated through volumes of data on Xelora's geology, atmosphere, and electromagnetic properties. The reports were cold and clinical, cataloguing Xelora's lifeless terrain, deep craters, and rock formations shaped by ancient, relentless forces. And yet, the more I analyzed, the more the planet revealed its secrets.

Xelora wasn't what it appeared to be. It was an anomaly in many ways. Its valleys were carved by forces unknown, the surface littered with energy readings that defied conventional physics. Atmospheric scans revealed a faint trace of elements that seemed to fluctuate in composition, as though the planet were breathing, pulsing with life. It was a subtle phenomenon, so faint that most researchers had dismissed it as a glitch in the data. But now, staring at the screen, I knew it was more than that. There was something alive on Xelora that didn't adhere to the rules of nature as we knew them.

The sporadic bursts of radiation emanating from the planet's surface were the most perplexing. They were weak, fleeting pulses, but seemed rhythmic, like a heartbeat. I stared at the frequency graph, my eyes darting between the data points. The bursts weren't natural; they were deliberate, a signal waiting to be deciphered. Could these pulses be what sustained her? Could they be why she was still alive, despite being so far from any source of nourishment or semblance of life?

"Impossible," I muttered, shaking my head. A barren planet couldn't harbour a living being, let alone allow her to communicate across the void. But if those pulses were intentional, someone—or something-was responsible for them. And if that was true, then the girl's presence on the planet might not be an anomaly after all.

I leaned forward, staring at the image of her still frozen on the screen. The faint glow of the monitor cast pale light across my face, accentuating the weariness in my eyes. She was alive, but just barely. Her body was limp, her movements weak, as if she were struggling against the weight of a thousand galaxies. And yet, there was something in those eyes, a glimmer of recognition, a spark that refused to be snuffed out.

I had to know more. I needed to understand what Xelora was, how it could sustain life, and how it was connected. The night stretched on, and I shifted between the telescope and the analysis console, searching for connections, cross-referencing data, and hoping for answers that seemed just out of reach.

Then, a sudden thought struck me. The encoded signals she had sent me, the ones that guided me to her position—what if they held more than just coordinates? What if they were more than cries for help? My pulse quickened. What if they were a map? A blueprint of sorts, pointing to something vital, something that could explain everything?

I opened the data logs and sifted through the encrypted transmissions. Each one was laced with noise, seemingly random bursts of static interwoven with words and fragments of phrases. I slowed down, examining each line, listening to how the static shifted in pitch, how the interference seemed to pulse in time with those strange radiation bursts. Patterns emerged, faint and elusive, like threads in a tapestry waiting to be woven together.

Hours turned into an indeterminate blur, the lines of code blending into the jagged, erratic beats on the screen. The fatigue was gnawing at me, but I pushed it aside, refusing to yield. Sleep was an indulgence I couldn't afford. My mind raced, weaving together the code and the data, making sense of the signals in ways I never thought possible. The realisation that Xelora was more than just a planet began to crystallise in my mind.

"Xelora isn't a planet," I whispered to myself. The thought reverberated through my mind, each word sharper than the last. What if Xelora were a conduit, a living entity that could bridge realities? A place where the laws of space and time were bent, where consciousness could transcend the boundaries of its physical shell? I leaned in, squinting at the screen as the signals twisted and shifted, revealing a hidden pattern I hadn't noticed before. Coordinates, yes, but also a language. The bursts of radiation and the encoded signals were a code I had just begun deciphering.

With a sudden surge of determination, I pieced together the message. It was embedded in the shifting static, a chorus of frequencies that told a story as old as time, one that defied reason and explanation. "Help me. You're my only hope," the words screamed from the screen, this time clear and precise. But it was more than a plea for help; it was a statement of trust, an acknowledgement that the girl believed I could save her. And I would.

The next step was critical. I had to confirm that the radiation pulses were connected to Xelora's energy signature. The analysis had been done, but it was time to test the theory. I calibrated the instruments to capture the pulses and followed them back to their source, their rhythm syncing with the encoded coordinates. The readings flared on the monitor, sending a thrill through me. The pulses came from the precise location where the girl lay.

But there was more. A faint, rhythmic signal embedded in the radiation bursts — almost like a heartbeat, but larger, grander. It was as if the entire planet were alive, resonating with her. The realization sent chills down my spine. The earth was sustaining her, but it was also holding her captive. The connection between them wasn't simple; it was complex, a relationship built on resonance and energy. Xelora kept her alive in a way that fed off her existence. It was both a prison and a lifeline.

I needed to understand how she could communicate with me. If the pulses were connected to the energy signature, her consciousness might use radiation as a conduit to project her voice and presence across space. It was the only explanation that fit. She wasn't just sending signals;

she was communicating through an intricate dance of energy that defied the known laws of physics.

The screen showed her image again; this time, it was clearer, as if she were reaching out from the depths of an abyss. Her eyes met mine, hollow and searching, yet filled with that same flicker of hope. I was no hero, no saviour, but to her, I was the only one who could reach her. And now, I understand. I could get her, not just with my voice, but with my mind, with everything I had. I would bridge the chasm between us.

The first step was to amplify the signal. I worked feverishly, rerouting power and recalibrating frequencies, pushing the equipment beyond its limits. The observatory trembled with the surge of energy, and for a moment, I was sure I had tried it too far. But then, her voice crackled through the static once more, weak but undeniably there.

"Time... slipping... away..." It was barely a whisper, but it pierced through the chaos in my mind. I turned to the console and reached for the receiver. My voice trembled as I spoke, raw with desperation.

"I'm here. You're not alone. I promise, I will find a way."

There was no immediate response. The signal wavered, shifting in and out like the edge of a dream. I glanced at the screen, watching the heat signature in the valley flicker as if it, too, were fighting to stay alive. A flicker of movement, almost imperceptible, the questions swirled in my mind as I stared at the flickering screen. How could she still be alive? How could she communicate with me across the unfathomable void of space? According to every scan and report, Xelora was barren, devoid of any breathable atmosphere or life-supporting elements. The stars, distant and indifferent, offered no answers. The girl was somewhere on that desolate surface, but her presence defied all logic.

The signals she had sent were a mystery in them—encoded, layered with noise, and yet infused with a precision that suggested intelligence far beyond mere coincidence. The coordinates, embedded in those signals, were precise now, marking a location deep within one of Xelora's endless valleys. But even with that clarity, the enigma of her existence remained. How was she surviving? And more perplexing, how was she speaking to me, reaching me across the unimaginable chasm of space?

I leaned back in my chair, rubbing my temples as exhaustion tugged at me. The observatory was silent save for the faint hum of equipment, a stark contrast to the turmoil in my mind. I needed answers; understanding the planet itself was the only way to get them.

Hours stretched into an unrecognizable blur of data and analysis. The steady hum of machinery filled the space, punctuated only by the soft whir of the control panel and the rhythmic pulse of the monitors. My fingers moved across the keyboard in a blur as I navigated through volumes of data on Xelora's geology, atmosphere, and electromagnetic properties. The reports were cold and clinical, cataloguing Xelora's lifeless terrain, deep craters, and rock formations shaped by ancient, relentless forces. And yet, the more I analyzed, the more the planet revealed its secrets.

Xelora wasn't what it appeared to be. It was an anomaly in many ways. Its valleys were carved by forces unknown, the surface littered with energy readings that defied conventional physics. Atmospheric scans revealed a faint trace of elements that seemed to fluctuate in composition, as though the planet were breathing, pulsing with life. It was a subtle phenomenon, so faint that most researchers had dismissed it as a glitch in the data. But now, staring at the screen, I knew it was more than that. There was something alive on Xelora that didn't adhere to the rules of nature as we knew them.

The sporadic bursts of radiation emanating from the planet's surface were the most perplexing. They were weak, fleeting pulses, but seemed rhythmic, like a heartbeat. I stared at the frequency graph, my eyes darting between the data points. The bursts weren't natural; they were deliberate, a signal waiting to be deciphered. Could these pulses be what sustained her? Could they be why she was still alive, despite being so far from any source of nourishment or semblance of life?

"Impossible," I muttered, shaking my head. A barren planet couldn't harbour a living being, let alone allow her to communicate across the void. But if those pulses were intentional, someone—or something—was responsible for them. And if that was true, then the girl's presence on the planet might not be an anomaly after all.

I leaned forward, staring at the image of her still frozen on the screen. The faint glow of the monitor cast pale light across my face, accentuating the weariness in my eyes. She was alive, but just barely. Her body was limp, her movements weak, as if she were struggling against the weight of a thousand galaxies. And yet, there was something in those eyes, a glimmer of recognition, a spark that refused to be snuffed out.

I had to know more. I needed to understand what Xelora was, how it could sustain life, and how it was connected to it. The night stretched on, and I shifted between the telescope and the analysis console, searching for connections, cross-referencing data, and hoping for answers that seemed just out of reach.

Then, a sudden thought struck me. The encoded signals she had sent me, the ones that guided me to her position—what if they held more than just coordinates? What if they were more than cries for help? My pulse quickened. What if they were a map? A blueprint of sorts, pointing to something vital, something that could explain everything?

I opened the data logs and sifted through the encrypted transmissions.

Each one was laced with noise, seemingly random bursts of static interwoven with words and fragments of phrases. I slowed down, examining each line, listening to how the static shifted in pitch, how the interference seemed to pulse in time with those strange radiation bursts. Patterns emerged, faint and elusive, like threads in a tapestry waiting to be woven together.

Hours turned into an indeterminate blur, the lines of code blending into the jagged, erratic beats on the screen. The fatigue was gnawing at me, but I pushed it aside, refusing to yield. Sleep was an indulgence I couldn't afford. My mind raced, weaving together the code and the data, making sense of the signals in ways I never thought possible. The realisation that Xelora was more than just a planet began to crystallise in my mind.

"Xelora isn't a planet," I whispered to myself. The thought reverberated through my mind, each word sharper than the last. What if Xelora were a conduit, a living entity that could bridge realities? A place where the laws of space and time were bent, where consciousness could transcend the boundaries of its physical shell? I leaned in, squinting at the screen as the signals twisted and shifted, revealing a hidden pattern I hadn't noticed before. Coordinates, yes, but also a language. The bursts of radiation and the encoded signals were a code I had only just begun to decipher.

With a sudden surge of determination, I pieced together the message. It was embedded in the shifting static, a chorus of frequencies that told a story as old as time, one that defied reason and explanation. "Help me. You're my only hope," the words screamed from the screen, this time clear and precise. But it was more than a plea for help; it was a statement of trust, an acknowledgement that the girl believed I could save her. And I would.

The next step was critical. I had to confirm that the radiation pulses were connected to Xelora's energy signature. The analysis had been done, but it was time to test the theory. I calibrated the instruments to capture the pulses and followed them back to their source, their rhythm syncing with the encoded coordinates. The readings flared on the monitor, sending a thrill through me. The pulses came from the precise location where the girl lay.

But there was more. A faint, rhythmic signal embedded in the radiation bursts — almost like a heartbeat, but larger, grander. It was as if the entire planet were alive, resonating with her. The realization sent chills down my spine. The earth was sustaining her, but it was also holding her captive. The connection between them wasn't simple; it was complex, a relationship built on resonance and energy. Xelora was keeping her alive, but doing so in a way that fed off her existence. It was both a prison and a lifeline.

I needed to understand how she could communicate with me. If the pulses were indeed connected to the energy signature, it meant that her consciousness might be using the radiation as a conduit to project her voice and presence across space. It was the only explanation that fit. She wasn't just sending signals; she was communicating through an intricate dance of energy that defied the known laws of physics.

The screen showed her image again; this time, it was clearer, as if she were reaching out from the depths of an abyss. Her eyes met mine, hollow and searching, yet filled with that same flicker of hope. I was no hero, no saviour, but to her, I was the only one who could reach her. And now, I understand. I could get her, not just with my voice, but with my mind, with everything I had. I would bridge the chasm between us.

The first step was to amplify the signal. I worked feverishly, rerouting power and recalibrating frequencies, pushing the equipment beyond its limits. The observatory trembled with the surge of energy, and for a moment, I was sure I had tried it too far. But then, her voice crackled through the static once more, weak but undeniably there.

"Time... slipping... away..." It was barely a whisper, but it pierced through the chaos in my mind. I turned to the console and reached for the receiver. My voice trembled as I spoke, raw with desperation.

"I'm here. You're not alone. I promise, I will find a way."

There was no immediate response. The signal wavered, shifting in and out like the edge of a dream. I glanced at the screen, watching the heat signature in the valley flicker as if it, too, were fighting to stay alive. A flicker of movement, almost imperceptible, crossed the monitor. I held my breath.

Her form shifted, reaching out for the paper she had dropped, now visible in the monitor's light. The words were clearer now, etched with a desperate precision that made my heart seize: *Help me. You're my only hope.*

The weight of those words pressed down on me, heavy and suffocating. I was nothing, I wasn't someone who could defy the laws of the universe or leap across the stars to save her.

The questions swirled in my mind as I stared at the flickering screen. How could she still be alive? How could she communicate with me across the unfathomable void of space? According to every scan and report, Xelora was barren, devoid of any breathable atmosphere or life-supporting elements. The stars, distant and indifferent, offered no answers. The girl was somewhere on that desolate surface, but her presence defied all logic.

The signals she had sent were a mystery in them—encoded, layered with noise, and yet infused with a precision that suggested intelligence far beyond mere coincidence. The coordinates, embedded in those signals, were precise now, marking a location deep within one of Xelora's endless valleys. But even with that clarity, the enigma of her existence remained. How was she surviving? And more perplexing, how was she speaking to me, reaching me across the unimaginable chasm of space?

I leaned back in my chair, rubbing my temples as exhaustion tugged at me. The observatory was silent save for the faint hum of equipment, a stark contrast to the turmoil in my mind. I needed answers; the only way to get them was to understand the planet itself.

Hours stretched into an unrecognizable blur of data and analysis. The steady hum of machinery filled the space, punctuated only by the soft whir of the control panel and the rhythmic pulse of the monitors. My fingers moved across the keyboard in a blur as I navigated through volumes of data on Xelora's geology, atmosphere, and electromagnetic properties. The reports were cold and clinical, cataloguing Xelora's lifeless terrain, deep craters, and rock formations shaped by ancient, relentless forces. And yet, the more I analyzed, the more the planet revealed its secrets.

Xelora wasn't what it appeared to be. It was an anomaly in many ways. Its valleys were carved by forces unknown, the surface littered with energy readings that defied conventional physics. Atmospheric scans revealed a faint trace of elements that seemed to fluctuate in composition, as though the planet were breathing, pulsing with life. It was a subtle phenomenon, so faint that most researchers had dismissed it as a glitch in the data. But now, staring at the screen, I knew it was more than that. There was something alive on Xelora that didn't adhere to the rules of nature as we knew them.

The sporadic bursts of radiation emanating from the planet's surface were the most perplexing. They were weak, fleeting pulses, but seemed rhythmic, like a heartbeat. I stared at the frequency graph, my eyes darting between the data points. The bursts weren't natural; they were deliberate, a signal waiting to be deciphered. Could these pulses be what sustained her? Could they be why she was still alive, despite being so far from any source of nourishment or semblance of life?

"Impossible," I muttered, shaking my head. A barren planet couldn't harbour a living being, let alone allow her to communicate across the void. But if those pulses were intentional, someone—or something—was responsible for them. And if that was true, then the girl's presence on the planet might not be an anomaly after all.

I leaned forward, staring at the image of her still frozen on the screen. The faint glow of the monitor cast pale light across my face, accentuating the weariness in my eyes. She was alive, but just barely. Her body was limp, her movements weak, as if she were struggling against the weight of a thousand galaxies. And yet, there was something in those eyes, a glimmer of recognition, a spark that refused to be snuffed out.

I had to know more. I needed to understand what Xelora was, how it could sustain life, and how it was connected. The night stretched on, and I shifted between the telescope and the analysis console, searching for connections, cross-referencing data, and hoping for answers that seemed just out of reach.

Then, a sudden thought struck me. The encoded signals she had sent me, the ones that guided me to her position—what if they held more than just coordinates? What if they were more than cries for help? My pulse quickened. What if they were a map? A blueprint of sorts, pointing to something vital, something that could explain everything?

I opened the data logs and sifted through the encrypted transmissions. Each one was laced with noise, seemingly random bursts of static interwoven with words and fragments of phrases. I slowed down, examining each line, listening to how the static shifted in pitch, how the interference seemed to pulse in time with those strange radiation bursts. Patterns emerged, faint and elusive, like threads in a tapestry waiting to be woven together.

Hours turned into an indeterminate blur, the lines of code blending into the jagged, erratic beats on the screen. The fatigue was gnawing at me, but I pushed it aside, refusing to yield. Sleep was an indulgence I couldn't afford. My mind raced, weaving together the code and the data, making sense of the signals in ways I never thought possible. The realisation that Xelora was more than just a planet began to crystallise in my mind.

"Xelora isn't a planet," I whispered to myself. The thought reverberated through my mind, each word sharper than the last. What if Xelora were a conduit, a living entity that could bridge realities? A place where the laws of space and time were bent, where consciousness could transcend the boundaries of its physical shell? I leaned in, squinting at the screen as the signals twisted and shifted, revealing a hidden pattern I hadn't noticed before. Coordinates, yes, but also a language. The bursts of radiation and the encoded signals were a code I had just begun deciphering.

With a sudden surge of determination, I pieced together the message. It was embedded in the shifting static, a chorus of frequencies that told a story as old as time, one that defied reason and explanation. "Help me. You're my only hope," the words screamed from the screen, this time clear and precise. But it was more than a plea for help; it was a statement of trust, an acknowledgement that the girl believed I could save her. And I would.

The next step was critical. I had to confirm that the radiation pulses were connected to Xelora's energy signature. The analysis had been done, but it was time to test the theory. I calibrated the instruments to capture the pulses and followed them back to their source, their rhythm syncing with the encoded coordinates. The readings flared on the monitor, sending a thrill through me. The pulses came from the precise location where the girl lay.

But there was more. A faint, rhythmic signal embedded in the radiation bursts — almost like a heartbeat, but larger, grander. It was as if the entire planet were alive, resonating with her. The realization sent chills down my spine. The earth was sustaining her, but it was also holding her captive. The connection between them wasn't simple; it was complex, a relationship built on resonance and energy. Xelora was keeping her alive, but doing so in a way that fed off her existence. It was both a prison and a lifeline.

I needed to understand how she could communicate with me. If the pulses were connected to the energy signature, her consciousness might be using the radiation as a conduit to project her voice and presence across space. It was the only explanation that fit. She wasn't just sending signals; she was communicating through an intricate dance of energy that defied the known laws of physics.

The screen showed her image again; this time, it was clearer, as if she were reaching out from the depths of an abyss. Her eyes met mine, hollow and searching, yet filled with that same flicker of hope. I was no hero, no saviour, but to her, I was the only one who could reach her. And now, I understand. I could get her, not just with my voice, but with my mind, with everything I had. I would bridge the chasm between us.

The first step was to amplify the signal. I worked feverishly, rerouting power and recalibrating frequencies, pushing the equipment beyond its limits. The observatory trembled with the surge of energy, and for a moment, I was sure I had tried it too far. But then, her voice crackled through the static once more, weak but undeniably there.

"Time... slipping... away..." It was barely a whisper, but it pierced through the chaos in my mind. I turned to the console and reached for the receiver. My voice trembled as I spoke, raw with desperation.

"I'm here. You're not alone. I promise, I will find a way."

There was no immediate response. The signal wavered, shifting in and out like the edge of a dream. I glanced at the screen, watching the heat signature in the valley flicker as if it, too, were fighting to stay alive. A flicker of movement, almost imperceptible, crossed the monitor. I held my breath.

Her form shifted, reaching out for the paper she had dropped, now visible in the monitor's light. The words were clearer now, etched with a desperate precision that made my heart seize: *Help me. You're my only hope.*

The weight of those words pressed down on me, heavy and suffocating. I was nothing, I wasn't someone who could defy the laws of the universe or leap across the stars to save her.

Crossed the monitor. I held my breath.

Her form shifted, reaching out for the paper she had dropped, now visible in the monitor's light. The words were clearer now, etched with a desperate precision that made my heart seize: *Help me. You're my only hope.*

The weight of those words pressed down on me, heavy and suffocating. I was nothing, I wasn't someone who could defy the laws of the universe or leap across the stars to save her.

Chapter 8:
The Research

The days blurred together as I threw myself into the research. Xelora, the mysterious planet, had left its mark on every study I reviewed. Yet, none of the pieces made sense—until now. The girl's presence, the strange signals, and the impossible conditions on Xelora were all hints of a bigger story, hidden beneath layers of time and destruction.

I dived into the archives, digging through every bit of data about Xelora. It had been discovered decades ago, and people were initially curious about it. But it was written off as a dull, but not a completely lifeless world—a rocky world with plenty of air, a place full of craters and silence. After it was catalogued, people moved on. Still, there were odd details in the records. Energy field readings didn't add up. Rhythmic signals were detected but brushed off as errors or interference. Back then, no one had taken them seriously.

But I am taking them seriously now.

The key was in the planet's electromagnetic data. The readings showed patterns that matched the signals the girl had sent. I ran tests, comparing the planet's historical data to the signals, and the results stunned me. The radiation bursts weren't random. They formed a sequence, a repeating loop.

Late one night, as exhaustion tugged at me, I found a breakthrough. It came from an old, forgotten file deep in the archives. The file was a telemetry log from an exploratory mission to Xelora. It had been dismissed as inconclusive then, but it held a critical clue. The log described a sudden, massive gravitational disturbance near the planet, so powerful that it disrupted the ship's instruments.

A black hole.

The thought sent chills down my spine. I searched for more data about the event. The black hole had passed close to Xelora thousands of years ago. Instead of destroying the planet, it created something bizarre. The immense gravity warped space and time around Xelora, leaving it partly connected to another dimension.

The researchers back then didn't know how to explain it. They suggested wild theories about alternate realities and time shifts, but those ideas were dismissed as nonsense. Now, though, everything was starting to make sense. The signals, the girl, and the strange conditions on Xelora revealed one truth: Xelora wasn't just a planet. It was a gateway.

I uncovered fragments of the civilisation that had once lived on Xelora. They were highly advanced, with technology far beyond what we could imagine. They had studied the black hole, perhaps even tried to control its power. But something went wrong. Their experiments tore their world apart, leaving Xelora as a tomb where time and space twisted together, trapping echoes of their existence in the planet itself.

And then there was the girl.

I stared at her faint image on my screen. She stood in a desolate valley on Xelora, her outline barely visible. How had she ended up there? Slowly, the answer came to me, pieced together from her signals and the whispers in her messages. She had stumbled into the loop—a moment when energy aligned just right, creating a bridge between Earth and Xelora. Her room on Earth had been the entry point, and she had unknowingly crossed over. But now the loop had closed behind her, leaving her trapped on the planet.

The truth hit me hard. Xelora wasn't just keeping her alive—it was feeding on her. The energy pulses and strange patterns weren't random. They were remnants of the lost civilisation, using her presence to sustain the loop.

Her message had been a desperate call for help. If I did nothing, the planet would drain her completely, leaving nothing behind but another echo in its endless void.

I turned back to my data. The black hole that had caused this disaster was also the key to fixing it. If I could manipulate the loop it created, I could reopen the bridge and bring her back. But this wasn't just about equations or simulations. It required more than knowledge. It needed creativity, determination, and the courage to face the unknown.

I took a deep breath, my fingers hovering over the keyboard. The task ahead was massive, but I couldn't give up. Xelora held secrets that defied everything we understood; within those secrets was the girl's salvation.

She had reached out to me, her voice crossing the impossible distance between our worlds. I couldn't let her down.

As I prepared to dive deeper into the research, one question burned in my mind: Could the same loop that had trapped her also be the key to bringing her home?

I didn't have the answers yet, but I knew one thing for sure. I would find a way. I would keep going for her and the mysteries of Xelora.

Chapter 9:
The Loops of Xelora

As I continued researching the strange phenomenon on Xelora, the girl's situation began to haunt me with increasing intensity. Deep down, I knew that this was no ordinary scientific anomaly. It wasn't just an error in my equipment, a miscalculation of the laws of physics. This was far beyond my understanding, bending the very fabric of reality itself.

The girl I had seen standing on that planet wasn't just lost in time; she was trapped in it. And there was something worse, something far more sinister at play. Xelora — this seemingly peaceful, distant world — suffered from a catastrophic time and space distortion. The more I investigated, the more I realized that this wasn't a simple case of a planet caught in some gravitational anomaly or an interstellar collision. No, what had happened to Xelora was far more profound, a wound in the fabric of the universe itself.

I had spent countless hours poring over the data, scouring through whatever information I could find about the planet. Then, I stumbled across an old document buried in the archives of the space agency I had access to: a report that mentioned the planet Xelora. At first, it appeared to be just another exploration report, filled with standard data about the planet's atmosphere, surface conditions, and mineral composition. But buried deep within its pages, I found something that sent a chill down my spine.

The report referred to a catastrophic event that had torn through Xelora's civilisation, warping both time and space in ways that the writers of the report could barely comprehend. As I read further, I discovered that Xelora had once been a thriving world, with its advanced civilisation and technology far beyond anything Earth had ever achieved. They had harnessed an energy source, a mysterious force that seemed to exist outside the normal laws of physics — a source of energy capable of manipulating time and space.

This energy had powered their cities, fueled their technology, and allowed them to bend the fabric of reality to their will. But something had gone wrong. The energy, which they had relied on for millennia, had begun to unravel the very structure of their world. No one knew exactly how or why it had happened, but the results were catastrophic. The energy source had destabilised, sending shockwaves throughout Xelora's atmosphere and causing a ripple effect that distorted the flow of time. The consequences were unimaginable.

Time itself had become unstable.

For Xelora, the planet was caught in an eternal cycle, a never-ending time loop. Time stretched and compressed at random intervals, creating a constant state of flux. Seconds could stretch into centuries, and years could pass in the blink of an eye. And all the while, the girl remained stuck in this anomaly. Every moment felt like an eternity for her, but for the rest of the universe — for Earth, for me — only a few moments had passed.

I leaned back in my chair, absorbing the implications of what I had uncovered. The girl I had been watching — the one trapped in her silent scream — was caught in a place where time itself had become distorted. The anomaly was so intense that it created a ripple effect, causing the space-time continuum around Xelora to warp and twist in unpredictable ways.

But there was more.

The ancient records I found in the ruins of Xelora's lost civilisation spoke of a mysterious energy force — an energy that had once been the lifeblood of their technology and their way of life. They called it the "Essence of Chrona" — a name that seemed to resonate with the planet's distorted relationship with time. The records were fragmented and incomplete, but from what I could gather, the Essence of Chrona was an almost magical energy capable of warping the universe's fundamental forces. It was not something the people of Xelora fully understood, but they had harnessed it to fuel their cities, manipulate time, and even travel through dimensions.

However, like all unchecked power, the Essence of Chrona had begun to decay. Its energy source had started to unravel, causing chaos across the planet. The distortion of time was only one of the many consequences. But a more troubling realisation hit me: the girl was the last living soul on Xelora. Or at least, she was the only one still trapped within the anomalous bubble of distorted time.

I shuddered as I processed this. If the Essence of Chrona was responsible for the time anomaly, and it was dying, then the girl's very existence—her torment, her call for help—was part of the collapse of Xelora's reality. The time loop was not a stable condition. It was deteriorating, and as the energy source continued to decay, the planet's connection to the rest of the universe would begin to sever. Soon, there would be no way for her to send any more messages or reach out for help.

I had to act. I couldn't sit idly by and watch this world, this girl, fade into oblivion.

The more I studied the ancient texts, the more I realised just how precious the Essence of Chrona had been to Xelora. The energy source had been both a blessing and a curse. It had allowed the civilisation to thrive, to master the forces of time, but it had also led to their downfall. The records spoke of the energy as a living force that was interconnected with the planet itself, its inhabitants, and even the very fabric of space-time around them. As the Essence of Chrona decayed, it had begun to pull apart the universe surrounding Xelora. The laws of physics were no longer predictable or stable. What had once been a world of prosperity had become a broken, fractured reality.

The people of Xelora, in their arrogance, had not foreseen the dangers of manipulating such a force. They had used it carelessly, thinking it would sustain them forever. But now, their world was dying, and with it, the last trace of their civilisation.

But the girl, the one who had appeared in my telescope, was different. She wasn't just a victim of the disaster. She was somehow preserved. Somehow, the last remnants of the Essence of Chrona had attached to her, allowing her to exist in this fractured time loop. The more I thought about it, the more it made sense. Her presence — her call for help — wasn't just the result of the collapse. It was a consequence of the dying energy itself. She was stuck, trapped between moments, between the past, the present, and the future.

The more I thought about her situation, the more I felt the task's urgency ahead. She had to be saved, or else her reality would continue to collapse, and she would be lost forever in the twisting void of time. I have to get back here anyhow.

I spent the next few days combing through every bit of data to know the exact timing of the next loop connecting the Planet to Earth. I could find on the Essence of Chrona that the more I learned, the clearer it became that the only way to save the girl was to stabilise the energy source and figure out about the next loop. But how could I, from Earth, stabilise an energy force that was located on a planet 50 light-years away? How could I even interact with something that existed in such a warped and distorted state?

I turned to every scientist, physicist, and engineer I knew, hoping to find a way to create a connection to the planet. I worked tirelessly on equations and theoretical models, hoping to find a way to reach Xelora and communicate with the energy force that had trapped the girl in its web. But the more I thought about it, the more impossible it seemed. The Essence of Chrona was something beyond anything that Earth had ever known — something that might not even obey the laws of our universe.

But there was one last possibility, a thought that had been gnawing at the back of my mind since the moment I first saw the girl. Could the telescope itself be a bridge — a means of reaching across the fabric of space-time, of communicating with Xelora? The idea seemed ludicrous, but there was no other explanation for how I had been able to see her in real-time. The telescope had somehow acted as a conduit for her image. Could I create a loop? The more I considered this possibility, the more I realised that it might be the only way. If the telescope was the key to connecting with the distorted reality of Xelora, then perhaps I could use it to send a signal, to reach out and stabilise the Essence of Chrona before it collapsed entirely.

I had no time to waste. Time was slipping away, just as the girl had said. And with every passing moment, Xelora was slipping further from the rest of the universe.

In the following weeks, I worked relentlessly, using every piece of equipment at my disposal. The data I had gathered on Xelora and the Essence of Chrona was becoming clearer, and the more I worked, the more I realised that there might be a way to intervene. I wasn't just an observer anymore. I was the last hope for the girl, Xelora, and everything that had once been, but the question remained: Could I save her? Or was I too late?

Chapter 10:
The Instantaneous Light

After weeks of intense observation and careful analysis, I arrived at a startling conclusion: the girl on Xelora was no longer experiencing time as we understand it. The decay of the Aetherium, an ancient and enigmatic energy source on the planet, had created a profound space-time distortion around her — a localized anomaly that defied conventional physics. The light carrying her image was not subject to the 50-year journey across the vast expanse of space. Instead, it arrived instantaneously, bridging the vast gulf between Xelora and my observatory as though the concept of distance had been erased. What I witnessed wasn't a relic of the past but the living present of a distorted reality.

This realisation, however, brought with it a chilling revelation: the Aetherium decay was far more dangerous than I initially suspected. The distortion it created wasn't stable; it was unravelling the fabric of time on Xelora. The planet's once-coherent temporal structure was being pulled into collapse, and its energy reserves were insufficient to maintain the balance. If nothing were done, Xelora would cease to exist, not as a shattered ruin but as an incoherent jumble of fragmented time. The girl wasn't merely stranded on a distant planet — she was trapped in a timeline that was collapsing in on itself.

My immediate priority became clear: I needed to communicate with her, to warn her of the danger and find a way to stabilise the anomaly. But how could I breach the boundaries of her fractured timeline? Ordinary communication methods were useless; radio waves, light signals, and even quantum entanglement could not traverse the chaotic distortion. I needed someone with expertise far beyond my own. I needed a sorcerer.

Enter Geha, a reclusive sorcerer for her unparalleled mastery of temporal manipulation and her profound knowledge of the Aetherium. Finding her was no small task. Her presence was whispered of in arcane circles, her whereabouts known only to a select few who guarded the secret fiercely. After weeks of searching and invoking every favour I was owed, I finally stood before her.

Geha was unlike anyone I had ever encountered. Draped in flowing robes that shimmered with a strange, otherworldly light, she radiated an aura of both wisdom and power. Her piercing eyes seemed to see through me and into the very fabric of my being. When I explained the situation, she listened intently, her expression inscrutable. When I finished, she nodded once.

"The Aetherium is a treacherous force," she said, voice low and resonant. "Its decay is not merely a scientific phenomenon but a cosmic wound. To mend it, we must weave the strands of time and space with precision and care. And to reach this girl, we must create a loop — a bridge between your reality and hers. But beware: such an act is not without consequences."

Despite her warning, I agreed. What choice do I have? Geha began her work immediately, drawing intricate sigils in the air with her hands, the symbols glowing and pulsating with a strange energy. She chanted in a language I didn't understand, her voice rising and falling in a hypnotic cadence. The room seemed to vibrate, the air growing thick with power. Then, with a final flourish, she turned to me.

"It is done," she said. "The loop is open. I have sent a message to the girl, using the instantaneous light as a medium. She will know you are trying to reach her. But there is more. I have done something else, something necessary to ensure our success."

Her words sent a shiver down my spine. "What did you do?" I demanded.

Geha hesitated, and for the first time, I saw a flicker of uncertainty in her eyes. "To stabilise the loop, I had to anchor it to a constant — a point of unchanging reality. I used a fragment of my essence. In doing so, I have tied myself to the anomaly. If the timeline collapses, I will be drawn into it as well. But there was no other way."

I was stunned. Her sacrifice was immense, but it also meant the stakes had risen exponentially. If we failed, it wouldn't just be the girl and Xelora that were lost. Geha's very existence was now intertwined with the success of our mission.

Over the next few days, we worked tirelessly to refine the loop and interpret the messages coming from the girl. Through the instantaneous light, fragmented images and disjointed words began to appear. She was aware of the distortion and terrified of what was happening around her. Her timeline was collapsing faster than anticipated, the Aetherium decay accelerating as the planet's energy reserves dwindled.

Geha's condition began to deteriorate. The strain of maintaining the loop was taking its toll; her connection to the anomaly was draining her vitality. She grew pale and weak, but her resolve never wavered. "We are close," she insisted, even as her voice faltered. "The girl has seen the message. She knows what must be done."

But then something unexpected happened. The girl, through the fragmented messages, began to communicate more clearly. She spoke of a presence on Xelora, an entity she called the Keeper. The Keeper, she claimed, was the guardian of the Aetherium, bound to protect it at all costs. The decay had weakened it, but it was still a formidable force. It had sensed our interference and was now actively working to sever the loop.

"This changes everything," Geha said, her expression grim. "The Keeper is not just a guardian but a part of the Aetherium itself. If it breaks the loop, the anomaly will collapse entirely. We must act quickly."

In a desperate bid to stabilise the situation, Geha and I devised a plan. Using the loop, we would send a stabilising pulse into the anomaly, a surge of energy designed to reinforce the timeline and counteract the Keeper's influence. It was a risky manoeuvre, one that required perfect timing and coordination.

The final phase of our plan was set into motion. Despite her weakened state, Geha poured every ounce of her power into the loop. The air crackled with energy as she chanted, her voice steady and commanding. The stabilising pulse surged through the loop, its brilliant light illuminating the room. For a moment, it worked. The anomaly's chaotic fluctuations began to subside, and the timeline showed signs of coherence.

But then the Keeper struck. A surge of dark energy erupted through the loop, lashing out with terrifying force. Geha screamed, her body convulsing as the energy tore through her. I watched in horror as she collapsed, her connection to the loop severed.

At that moment, I thought all was lost. But then, through the light of the loop, the girl appeared. Her image was more transparent than ever, her eyes filled with determination. She reached out, her hand passing through the distortion to touch Geha's fallen form. A surge of energy flowed between them, the girl's presence stabilising the loop in a way I couldn't comprehend.

"Thank you," she said, her voice resonating through the anomaly. "I understand now. The Keeper's power comes from fear and isolation. But together, we can overcome it."

With her guidance, I reactivated the stabilising pulse, this time with the girl's energy augmenting it. The Keeper's dark presence began to waver, its power diminishing as the timeline stabilised. Finally, with a final burst of light, the anomaly collapsed, leaving a calm and coherent reality behind.

Geha lay motionless on the floor, her breathing shallow but steady. The girl's image faded, but her voice lingered. "You saved me," she said. "And in doing so, you saved Xelora. The Aetherium decay has been halted. Its power can now be renewed."

As the loop closed, I turned to Geha, her sacrifice etched into every line of her face. She had given everything to save a world she had never seen, a girl she had never met. And in doing so, she had reminded me of the boundless potential of courage and compassion.

Xelora was safe, the anomaly resolved. But the experience had changed me forever. The mysteries of the Aetherium and the courage of those who fought to protect it would remain with me always, a testament to the power of connection and the enduring strength of the human spirit.

Chapter 11:
The Impossible Choice

The closer I understood what was happening, the more desperate I became. If the Aetherium died, so would the girl. And worse, the ripple effects of Xelora's collapsing time would extend across the universe. The fabric of space-time was beginning to stretch thin, and reality itself was starting to fray.

I knew there was only one solution — I had to reach her. I had to connect our realities somehow, bypass the light-years that separated us, and pull her out of her world before it collapsed.

But how?

The answer came from an ancient, cryptic message from the Xeloran records. It spoke of a technology that could stabilize the Aetherium: a device capable of locally reversing the flow of time. However, it required an immense amount of energy — the kind that could only be found in the core of a dying star.

I remember the day I found my grandfather's old diary — its leather cover cracked with age, the pages filled with strange diagrams and urgent scrawls in his looping hand. He had always spoken in riddles, obsessed with "the deeper pulse of the universe." But as I turned the fragile pages, a realisation struck me with terrifying clarity: he had known about the Aetherium. This elusive, unstable energy flickered at the edge of space and time. He wrote of a device that could stabilise it, even reverse the flow of time. He called it the Trinity Core. According to him, it wasn't just a machine, but a convergence of three elements: the Singularity Chamber, which could resonate with quantum fluctuations and act as a container for raw Aetherium; the Memory Prism, a crystal designed to hold emotional echoes and memories as a temporal key; and the Soul Anchor, the final piece that required a living soul — one willing to be tethered to the device to complete the loop. As I traced his notes, I realized he had built it once.

I turned the pages beneath a dim lamp in his forgotten study, and something shifted. Tucked between two entries was a faded sketch of this room, marked with a faint X on the back wall. My pulse quickened. I moved the old shelves aside, fingers trembling, and knocked until I heard the hollow sound I hadn't known I was waiting for. Behind a loose panel, hidden for decades, was a sealed compartment. Inside lay a bundle wrapped in oilcloth — the true heart of his legacy.

Within it, detailed blueprints, fragments of crystal, and a note in his unmistakable hand: *"The Aetherium is unstable. The Trinity Core is the only way. Singularity. Memory. Soul. But beware — the final anchor must be willing."* My grandfather had discovered a way to stabilize the Aetherium and reverse the flow of time, and built the device.

On one page, stained with what looked like a burn mark, he had drawn the layout of the room I stood in, with a cryptic X near the far wall beneath the tall bookshelf. My heart pounded as I moved the shelf aside, revealing cracked plaster behind it. I knocked once, twice — until a hollow echo answered. There was something inside.

With a chisel and shaking hands, I chipped away at the wall until a piece gave way, revealing a small compartment lined with velvet and wrapped in layers of foil that shimmered faintly in the dark. Inside was a bundle — sealed tight and humming softly, as if alive. A note: *"To the one who seeks, this is the Trinity Core. It is not merely a machine, but a convergence of power: the Singularity Chamber to hold the Aetherium, the Memory Prism to align time's flow, and the Soul Anchor... that is the sacrifice. I couldn't do it. But maybe you can."* My grandfather hadn't lost his mind — he had hidden the future in this room. And now, it was calling to me.

The Trinity Core. I unwrapped it with care, expecting a dead, dormant artefact. But to my astonishment, it was humming—alive. Its central crystal spun slowly, surrounded by tiny arcs of silent electricity. It was already charged. It hadn't decayed or worn down after all these years, sealed in darkness, untouched by time. It waited. That was the most unsettling part. It had been waiting for me. The diary had spoken of immense energy needs, of sacrifices to activate the Soul Anchor… yet here it was, humming softly in my hands, already full as if it had been drawing from something else entirely. As if it *knew* I would come.

The Trinity Core was, like I'd imagined. It filled almost the entire hidden chamber. It was volumetric — nearly ten feet tall, built with a skeletal frame of dark alloy and glowing, transparent conduits running through its structure like veins. A rotating crystal sphere hovered in its heart, suspended in mid-air by forces I couldn't understand. Tubes spiralled outward from it, connecting to prongs embedded in the chamber walls. The room was designed around it, almost like a containment field or a shrine.

And the most shocking part — it was active. Despite the decades sealed away, it thrummed softly with life, as if the Aetherium within it had been feeding on time itself, no fuel source. No decay. Just that eerie, constant hum, like the whisper of something ancient and waiting. My grandfather hadn't built it — he had buried a sleeping giant. And now, it was awake.

The moment I activated the device, the universe around me seemed to distort. Time fractured, light bent, and for a fleeting moment, I was no longer on Earth. I found myself standing on the land of Xelora, with the girl before me, her eyes wide with recognition.

As I stood before the colossal form of the Trinity Core, its soft hum deepening into a rhythmic pulse, something in my grandfather's clicked into place. One fragmented entry had mentioned "Xelora" — the cradle of the first Aetherium breach. Unt" l now, I'd imagined it was metaphorical. But the machine wasn't charged — it was connected, alive, feeding off something beyond this world. A signal pulsed from its core, a resonance not of Earth, but of something far older and far away. With a cold shiver, I realised that the device was linked to the Aetherium fields of Xelora, a distant planet once thought to be only a myth in scattered scientific rumours and lost cosmic charts.

There was no choice. If Xelora's energy sustained the Trinity Core, Xelora's answers — maybe even control — lay there. I initiated the device's tradevice tool, encoded deep within its structure. Space around me warped, folded inward, and time flexed like breath held tight. In the next moment, I was no longer on Earth. The air was heavier, charged, and the horizon shimmered with unfamiliar colours. I had arrived on Xelora — the world my grandfather had whispered. I was there with that girl; I could not believe she was as genuine as the sun.

The planet was collapsing, but I had one final chance to get there. As I held the device, the last remnants of the Aetherium began to stabilise. Time was starting to correct itself, but it wouldn't be wouldn'tore the final collapse would occur. She was not ready to come with me.

Chapter 12:
The Final Light

Staring at the vibrant, alien landscape while getting lost in thoughts where the girl towered over me, I took a moment to capture my racing heart before looking at the pale sun, basking in its last rays. I noticed she was standing next to me, but in complete silence, looking and feeling incredibly assured. Her choice had been made. Together, shaking with anticipation, we clicked the button.

The lights began to shimmer, and a pitch low enough to be barely heard started filling the air until, out of the blue, it turned into a gigantic howl. The planet's energy was torn apart due to the Aetherium's collapse. Afterwards, everything began shaking violently, and the skies broke into dominantly shining colours until the planet was enveloped in a monumentally immense flash of light.

My heart was beating out of my chest. It was only then that I noticed I was back on Earth. For now, all I will need, alone here, sprawled over my previously owned telescope. Noticing the cool breeze, I was greeted with a chill down my spine. With a newfound urge, I turned the telescope around, only to be met with a sombre sight of being unable to recognise it.

Xelora had shattered without a single word; the girl was gone. I wonder if a little amount of scream or whisper. Once brought back into reality, I begin asking myself,

'Where, oh! Where does this leave us?' and 'How do I respond to everything thrown at me?' The weak tonal light from the moon was painfully bland. Beyond unbearable. Having anything remotely friendlier than the freezing air can't explain how horrible it felt. Furthermore, skimming around the edges of time itself.

However, as I gazed into the nothingness that once was vibrantly bursting with life, a solitary concern resonated throughout me: Could it be that the girl was really gone? Was it all a dream?

What if she had bypassed the limits of time and space and crossed the boundaries of reality, venturing into an unseen dimension? Could she still exist as a spirit lingering between cosmos, twirling outside the boundaries of recollection and science? Perhaps I will never discover this.

www.ingramcontent.com/pod-product-compliance
Lightning Source LLC
LaVergne TN
LVHW061551070526
838199LV00077B/6997